morssay 99

DATE DUE

FE 18'93	SEP 1 9 1997		
FEB 17 '94			
MAR 1 8 1994			
JY 1 5'95			
SEP 9 '9?			
MAY 1 '98			
	261-2500		Printed in USA

SIMON SAYS

Story and Pictures by

BILL MORRISON

LITTLE, BROWN AND COMPANY
BOSTON   TORONTO

jP

To Betsy Isele,

for giving Turtle

his big day

FIRST EDITION

Library of Congress Cataloging in Publication Data

Morrison, Bill, 1935.
   "Simon says".

   Summary: A group of animals, including a turtle, a
giraffe, and a hippopotamus, who decide to play at
taking turns imitating each other, find out that they
are not all good at the same things.
   [1. Animals — Fiction.   2. Play — Fiction]   I. Title.
PZ7.M82925Si 1983   [E]   83-9431
ISBN 0-316-58475-4

WOR
*Published simultaneously in Canada
by Little, Brown & Company (Canada) Limited*
PRINTED IN THE UNITED STATES OF AMERICA